The Puppy who Ran Away

Holly Webb

Illustrated by Sophy Williams

LITTLE TIGER

LONDON

For Alice

STRIPES PUBLISHING LIMITED
An imprint of the Little Tiger Group
1 Coda Studios, 189 Munster Road, London SW6 6AW

Imported into the EEA by Penguin Random House Ireland,
Morrison Chambers, 32 Nassau Street, Dublin D02 YH68

A paperback original
First published in Great Britain in 2021

Text copyright © Holly Webb, 2021
Illustrations copyright © Sophy Williams, 2021
Author photograph © Charlotte Knee Photography

ISBN: 978-1-78895-303-0

A CIP catalogue record for this book is available from the British Library.

Printed and bound in the UK.

MIX
Paper from
responsible sources
FSC® C020471

The Forest Stewardship Council® (FSC®) is a global, not-for-profit
organization dedicated to the promotion of responsible forest management
worldwide. FSC defines standards based on agreed principles for
responsible forest stewardship that are supported by environmental, social,
and economic stakeholders. To learn more, visit www.fsc.org

10 9 8 7 6 5 4 3 2 1

Chapter One

Isabella picked at her breakfast. She wasn't really hungry but she knew that Gran and Grandad were keeping an eye on her. She took a bite of toast to make them feel better.

Grandad stroked her hair. "You're ever so quiet."

Isabella swallowed hard, trying to get the mouthful of toast to go down her throat. She smiled at Grandad but it came out a bit wrong.

Gran looked at her anxiously. "It's going to be all right, Isabella. I know it's a strange day but it'll be so nice to see your mum again, won't it?"

Isabella nodded, since she couldn't get any words to come out around the dry toast. Gran was right – she had missed Mum so much over the last two weeks and she was desperate to see her. She'd loved being at Gran and Grandad's while Mum was on her honeymoon in Greece, but she'd never been away from Mum for so long and she wanted to go home.

The problem was, she wasn't going home. Not really.

She was going to Mike's house. It

was supposed to be Mum's house and her house now too but it just wasn't. It belonged to Mike and his son, Sam. Mum had explained that it made sense for them all to live there together after the wedding, because Mike's house was bigger than theirs. There was a lovely bedroom that Isabella could have and Mum had promised she could paint it any colours she liked. Isabella liked her old bedroom. It was rather grubby and small but she didn't care. It was hers.

She was trying *so hard* to be happy, because her mum was happy. Mum kept smiling all the time and she sang while she was cooking, and when she was on the phone to Mike she was always laughing. Isabella really liked Mike too. He was funny and he told silly jokes, silly enough to make Isabella cry with laughter sometimes... It was just a lot – suddenly having a stepdad and a stepbrother and a new house and a new bedroom.

"Finish off your breakfast, Isabella," Grandad said. "You haven't got long before your mum gets here to take you to Mike's house ... I mean, your house..."

Gran gave him a look and then turned to Isabella. "She said she'd be here about nine. Have you got everything packed?"

"Yes," Isabella murmured at last. "I put my things in the hallway." She'd only had a small bag of clothes and her school things with her at Gran and Grandad's – everything else from her bedroom had already been moved.

On Monday, she'd be going to school from the new house, instead of walking with Gran and Grandad. They quite often took her to school when Mum was on a shift at her care home, and of course they'd taken her every day while Mum and Mike were away.

That was one good thing about moving – Mike and Sam's house was close to school, and her best friend Beatrice lived next door. Her mum and Beatrice's mum had agreed they were old enough to walk to school together now, on their own.

When Isabella and Beatrice had suggested it, Mike had told their mums that Sam used to walk to school on his own in Year Five, no problem. Sam was in Year Seven now, so he went to the secondary school, in the other direction. Isabella had sort of known him even before his dad started dating her mum, since their school wasn't very big. She'd never imagined she'd end up sharing a house with him, though. It was going to be so strange, after it had been just her and Mum for so long.

Isabella froze in her seat as she heard a car pull up. A moment later, the doorbell rang. Isabella forgot all about the weirdness, almost tipping over her chair as she rushed to answer the door.

Mum swept Isabella up into a huge hug as soon as the door opened. "Oh, I've missed you!" she said, laughing into Isabella's curly hair.

"Me too! Did you have a good time?"

"It was wonderful. We'll have to go back there one day, all of us."

Isabella pressed her face into Mum's shoulder. That was another weird thing – family holidays were going to be the four of them now.

"So, ready to go to the house?" Mum asked gently.

"Yes," Isabella whispered. "I'll get my stuff."

Grandad was already picking up her bags and passing them out to Mike, while Gran kissed her goodbye.

"Sam's looking forward to seeing you," Mike said as they got in the car, but Isabella thought he was probably just being polite. Mike and Mum had arranged several days out for the new family, so she and Sam could get to know each other before the wedding, but she hadn't seen him while her mum and Mike were in Greece. He'd stayed at his house – *their* house, she had to try and think of it as their house – while his dad was away. His nana had come to stay and look after him.

"Oh, and you can meet Honey!" Mum said enthusiastically. "Sam's puppy … remember I told you about her? She's lovely." She turned round to smile at Isabella, and Isabella nodded.

Mum had told her that Mike and Sam had adopted a puppy from the animal shelter about a month ago. Isabella hadn't had a chance to meet her yet but she was really looking forward to it. She loved dogs but she had never had one. Mum had been worried about leaving a dog alone at home when she was at work. Living at Mike and Sam's house was going to be weird but Isabella kept on telling herself, *At least now I get a dog…*

"I expect she'll look loads bigger now," Mike said. "She was only about eight weeks old when we brought her home from the shelter. I've got a feeling she's going to be huge when she's fully grown."

"Mum said Honey was a spaniel. Or mostly a spaniel?" Isabella said, leaning forwards a little.

"The shelter weren't absolutely sure but they reckoned a bit of spaniel and maybe a bit of Golden Retriever. She's a lovely golden brown colour."

"And she's got beautiful fluffy ears," Mum put in. "But the most important thing is that she's so friendly and sweet!"

"We could all go for a walk with her this afternoon," Mike suggested. "Here we are, look. Oh, there's my mum watching out for us." He parked the car and waved to a lady standing by the window at the front of the house.

Isabella slowly got out of the car, watching the front door open. Sam's nana was waving at them but Isabella didn't really know what to do. She didn't feel like she could just walk into the house. She went round to the boot and picked up her bags.

"It's OK," Mum said, coming to stand next to her. She put an arm round Isabella's shoulders. "I know it feels strange. Take it slowly, all right?"

Isabella nodded gratefully and then laughed out loud. Sam had suddenly appeared at the door, with his arms full of fluffy golden dog. Honey was wriggling and squirming and squeaking with excitement – it looked like Sam was having a hard job holding on to her.

Mum laughed too. "I told you she was gorgeous, didn't I? Wow, she really has grown…" She shepherded Isabella along the gravel drive to the house, and Isabella tried to smile and look pleased to be there. Actually, it was loads easier than she'd thought it would be, since there was Honey acting as though meeting her was the most amazing thing that had ever happened. The puppy was leaning out of Sam's arms, trying to reach Isabella to lick her, and her tail was wagging so fast it was thumping against Sam's hoodie.

"Hey…" Sam said. He seemed rather embarrassed, but he made Honey wave a soft golden paw at Isabella. "This is Honey. Is it OK if I put her down? You're not scared of her, are you? I don't think I can hold her much longer."

Isabella shook her head. "I'm not scared. I love dogs."

"Oh good." Sam looked relieved. "Your mum said you did but I was still worried. We're trying to train her not to jump up but she gets a bit bouncy around new people." He backed into the hall to get out of the way of the bags and crouched on the floor with Honey. "Shh, calm down…"

Isabella watched them doubtfully. Was it OK to get on the floor with Honey too? She didn't want to go

too fast and frighten the puppy. Then
Honey squirmed out of Sam's arms at
last and lay across Isabella's trainers,
wriggling about and waving her paws
in the air. She gazed up at Isabella with
huge, dark eyes and whined hopefully.

Sam laughed. "She likes you!"

Isabella couldn't stop the smile
spreading over her face. Honey was so
soft and warm and wriggly
on her feet. She kneeled
down and let Honey
lick her hands
and climb into
her lap. Maybe
everything
was going
to be all
right.

Honey nuzzled her nose under the girl's chin with little whines of pleasure. A new person! And this girl was scratching her ears now, her favourite spot. Honey sighed happily and slumped into Isabella's lap.

"She *definitely* likes you," Sam said, sounding a bit surprised, and Honey looked up at him, hoping that he'd crouch down and fuss over her too. He stayed standing though, watching as the girl rubbed Honey's ears, and whispered how beautiful she was. Honey gave the girl one last lick to her chin and hopped out of her lap, trotting over to lean against Sam's legs instead.

Chapter Two

"Sam, why don't you take Isabella out on your walk too?" Mike suggested, and Isabella looked round hopefully. She'd been doing her numeracy homework at the kitchen table. Over the last couple of weeks living at the new house she'd discovered that Mike was really helpful with maths. He was emptying the dishwasher but he kept stopping to lean over her shoulder and point out where she'd got mixed up.

"She's doing her homework," Sam said. Honey was bouncing round his feet – she obviously knew exactly what the lead in his hand meant.

"I've nearly finished. I'm on the last one!" Isabella said, scribbling frantically. "There!"

She looked up at Sam and she was almost sure he sighed. She didn't really mind, though. He'd been OK with suddenly having her around all the time and Isabella knew it must be as strange for him as it was for her. Every so often Sam wandered into the kitchen or the living room and looked totally shocked to find her there, almost as if he'd forgotten about her for a moment. It was probably good that they were at different schools, she thought, so they weren't on top of each other the whole time.

Was it too much, wanting to go for a walk with them? Honey was definitely Sam's dog. Isabella got to stroke her and fuss over her but Sam was the one who fed her and he was in charge of her walks. Isabella glanced at him sideways, trying to see if he was annoyed, but he looked OK. They had been on a few family dog walks in the couple of weeks since she'd moved in but Isabella hadn't been out with just Sam and Honey yet. She was a bit jealous that Sam was allowed to go out all on his own but he was two years older than she was and he had his own phone in case he got into trouble.

She dashed into the hallway to put on her trainers and Honey followed her. The puppy was whining with excitement and trying hard to lick Isabella's face as she sat on the bottom step doing up her laces.

"Uuughh!" Isabella giggled. "I'll never be ready if you keep doing that. Get off my shoelaces, silly." She put her arm round Honey and then rubbed her cheek against the little dog's soft ears.

"Ready?" Sam asked.

Isabella nodded. "Where are we going? The park?" All four of them had been to walk Honey in the park a few times now. Honey loved watching the ducks on the lake.

"Me and Honey usually go to the woods. Bell's Copse – there's a cut-through round the corner."

Isabella stared at him blankly and Sam looked surprised. "You've never been there? It's great. It's small but there's lots of paths and they cross over each other, so it feels bigger. There's a stream as well. Dad used to take me there to build dens and stuff." Sam leaned down to clip on Honey's lead. "Come on, Honey. Walk!"

Isabella followed them out of the front door, admiring the way Sam coaxed Honey along. The puppy was enthusiastic about walking but she wanted to stop and sniff every stone, every lamp post, every patch of weeds. It took them a good ten minutes to get to the end of the street. Sam kept pretending to sigh and roll his eyes, making Isabella laugh. Then he led them along a little alleyway with tall fences either side.

"Oh! You can see these trees from the garden!" Isabella said, spotting a sign at the end of the alley that said Bell's Copse.

"Yeah, we're lucky it's so close. Honey, look! Trees! Come on!"

Honey yapped excitedly and

managed to get about ten metres down the alley without stopping to sniff anything, which was a record.

The woods had a big patch of grass in front that was ankle-deep on Sam and Isabella but Honey was practically up to her nose. She went galloping through the grass with her ears flying, doing a great bouncing leap every few steps so she could see where she was going.

"Can we let her off the lead?" Isabella asked, jogging along next to Honey and Sam.

Sam shook his head. "Not yet. Maybe when she's been to more training classes. She's still not very good at coming back when she's called." He looked around as if he thought someone might be listening and then said, "Don't tell Dad but she slipped out of the front door once while he was away. Nana answered the door to the postman and Honey went right between her feet. She was halfway down the street before I caught up with her." He shuddered and Isabella frowned worriedly.

"Wow, that must have been scary."

"Yeah. So I'm keeping the lead on for the minute." He gave Isabella a considering look. "But you can hold it if you like."

Isabella stared up at him in surprise. She'd been hoping for ages to be allowed to walk Honey herself but she hadn't been brave enough to ask. Honey was Sam's dog and she didn't want to get in the way. "Really? Yes,

please! I'll be ever
so careful!"

Sam handed
over the lead.
"Just don't let
her pull it out
of your hand.
She's only little
but she can
pull hard if she gets excited."

Isabella nodded. She gripped the
lead so tightly her knuckles started to
go white but it was so brilliant, feeling
Honey dance and tug at the end of
it. Isabella felt scared and happy and
responsible all at the same time.

"Come on, I'll show you the stream."
Sam led them through the gate into
the wood itself and Isabella looked

round, surprised at how shady and cool it was under the trees. She sniffed at the strange woody smell – trees and damp earth. Sam was right - they were so lucky to have a place like this so close. There were even a few foxgloves on the slope they were passing now. Honey buried her nose in the long green leaves and sneezed.

"There, look." Sam stopped, pointing to a little stream trickling along below them. "It's not very big but Honey loves splashing in it." The puppy was peering down at the water and wagging her tail wildly. She pulled a little, as if she was planning to jump in but Sam gave Isabella's bright white trainers a worried look and put his hand on the lead. "Maybe not in those.

We can do it another day."

Isabella smiled. Another day. That meant another walk.

Honey yawned and stretched, then peered around the kitchen. It was definitely breakfast time, she reckoned. Sam would be coming to feed her soon, and then he'd get his own breakfast and talk to her while she ate her biscuits. Honey scrambled out of her basket – it was still a bit big for her – and trotted over to scratch at the kitchen door.

Nothing. She tried again, a little louder, and this time she did hear footsteps – but it didn't sound like

Sam. These footsteps were lighter. Honey gave a slow, puzzled wag of her tail and sat down to watch the door.

It opened just a crack and someone peered round. Honey thumped her tail on the kitchen floor and panted happily at Isabella.

"Hey… Are you hungry? Is that why you were scratching? I came down to watch TV but I don't think Sam's up yet." Isabella slipped into the kitchen.

Honey closed her eyes blissfully as Isabella scratched behind her ears. Then she got up and padded over to look meaningfully at her empty food bowl.

Isabella glanced back at the kitchen door uncertainly and nibbled her thumbnail. Honey watched the girl with her head on one side. What

was the matter? Why did she look so
worried?

Then at last Isabella went to the
cupboard where Honey knew her
food was kept. Honey sped up her
tail wagging and gave a little bark of
encouragement. She watched eagerly
as Isabella pulled the bag of puppy
food out of the cupboard and reached
inside it for the measuring cup.

"Hey! What are you doing?"

Honey whirled round, her ears
twitching in confusion, and Isabella
jumped, nearly spilling the food bag.
Sam was standing by the door in his
pyjamas. She wanted to race to him
so he could make a fuss of her the way
he always did when he came down
in the mornings. But Sam's voice was

different – sharp and strange. He came stomping across the kitchen towards her and Isabella, and Honey thought he even smelled different. She whined anxiously and backed away a little as he stood over Isabella. This wasn't her Sam...

"You don't feed her!" Sam snapped. "She's my dog!"

"I'm sorry…" Isabella faltered. "She was whining. I thought she was hungry…"

"I was coming. Just leave her alone!"

"Stop shouting," Isabella said, folding her arms. "I was only trying to help. You're scaring her, look!"

He glared at her. "I didn't do anything! You're the one stealing my dog."

Honey watched miserably as Isabella dashed out of the kitchen, and Sam grabbed the bag of food and the cup. She didn't understand what had just happened but she hated the hot, fizzing anger that was filling the room. The biscuits rattled sharply into her metal bowl but somehow Honey wasn't hungry any more.

Chapter Three

Isabella didn't tell Mum or Mike what Sam had said to her that morning. She didn't want anybody else to know. She just buried it down deep and tried to stay out of her stepbrother's way. But Mum and Mike always encouraged them to spend time together at the weekends, so it was tricky. Isabella had to keep making up extra homework so she could stay in her room without anyone asking her why. She was pretty sure that Mum was giving her worried looks, but she didn't say anything.

Isabella was trying to avoid Honey too and she hated it. She didn't want Sam to get upset with her again and she supposed he was a little bit right. Honey *was* his dog, even if she had only been trying to help. If Honey had been hers, she might have been upset too. Although she was sure she wouldn't have been so mean about it.

Honey didn't seem to realize that Isabella was trying to stay away from her. Isabella supposed it wouldn't make much sense to a puppy. Only the day before they'd been on that walk together to the woods and Sam had let her hold Honey's lead.

On Monday before school Honey scurried between Sam and Isabella as usual, watching eagerly for dropped toast crusts. Isabella tried not to pay her any attention but how was she supposed to ignore those gentle nudges from Honey's damp nose? The nudges were getting harder and harder, and then Honey put her paws up on Isabella's knee and licked her arm hopefully.

Isabella darted a worried glance at Sam but she didn't think he'd noticed. He was gobbling his breakfast and trying to message someone on his phone at the same time. Isabella slipped Honey the corner of her piece of toast and gently pushed the puppy back down. She wanted to rub Honey's ears and tell her she was gorgeous but she knew she'd better not, just in case.

Isabella swallowed a sigh. How was she supposed to live in the same house as a gorgeous puppy and not pay her any attention?

Isabella was quiet all day at school, trying to work out what she was going to do about Honey and Sam.

"Why are you walking so slowly?" Beatrice asked as they came round the corner into their road. "You've hardly said anything all day. What's the matter?"

Isabella sighed. She still hadn't told

anyone about her fight with Sam the day before but maybe it would help to talk about it. "You have to promise not to tell your mum, because she'd tell mine," she warned.

Beatrice nodded. "OK."

"It sounds so stupid…" Isabella said. "I got up early yesterday, earlier than anyone else. I thought I'd go and watch TV for a bit. But when I went downstairs Honey was awake and she was scratching at the kitchen door, so I went to say hello. And then she was hungry. She was acting like she was starved! So … I got her food out." She heaved another huge sigh. "That's when Sam walked in and started shouting at me. He said I was trying to steal her!"

"Oh, that's not fair! You were only trying to help!"

Isabella shrugged. "Yeah. But I keep thinking, if it was the other way round I'd probably feel the same… He has to share everything now. His house. His dad." She sniffed. "But he didn't have to shout at me!"

"Ignore him!" Beatrice said. "He'll get used to it. Anyway, if he's mean you can come round to mine, OK?"

Isabella nodded and sniffed again. Beatrice had made her feel a bit better but she still had to share a house with Sam – and Honey.

Honey lifted her head from her basket. Was that the door? She loved it when Sam and Isabella got home from school. She yelped delightedly and raced down the hallway. Mike was home during the day but he was always too busy to play with Honey for long. He took her for a walk every lunchtime but for the rest of the day Honey snoozed in her basket, chewed her toys, and wandered around the garden.

But now Isabella was home! She bounced next to the front door until Mike came to open it and then she flung herself at Isabella, desperate for love and ear-rubs. Isabella shut the door quickly, which was a pity, because

Honey would have liked to go out and explore, but then Isabella crouched next to her. She let Honey sniff her and lick her hands.

"You're so lovely, yes you are. Aren't you a good dog?" Isabella whispered, smoothing her hand over the velvet fur on the top of Honey's head. Honey closed her eyes blissfully and leaned against Isabella, breathing in the sunny smells of outdoors.

"I shouldn't be doing this but I can't not love you, can I?" Isabella sighed. "Not when you're so sweet. But we have to pretend when Sam's around, OK?"

Honey could hear the sadness in Isabella's voice and she leaned harder against her legs, rubbing her muzzle against Isabella's knee.

"Yes, you're a good girl— Oh!"

Honey sprang up, hearing the
crunch of gravel, and barked excitedly.
Now Sam was back as well and she
had both of them. Sam was her first
person, her best, but she adored
Isabella too, and she loved it when they
both played with her.

As the key clicked in the lock,
Isabella jumped up. Honey glanced
round nervously. What was wrong?

All of a sudden she remembered that angry, frightening moment in the kitchen the day before and she let out a tiny whine as the door opened. She tried to wiggle back behind Isabella's legs to be safe but Isabella pushed her away.

Honey stood uncertainly in the middle of the hall, hating this strange feeling. She tucked her tail between her legs and stared up at Sam, her ears flattened with worry.

"Isabella…"

Isabella looked up as Sam stuck his head round her bedroom door. She had hurried away from Honey as soon as she heard him coming home but she wasn't sure she'd got away with it. She had a feeling it was obvious she'd been fussing over the puppy.

"Yes?" she asked, trying not to sound guilty.

"Look, I'm sorry."

Isabella's eyes widened, and then she couldn't help smiling as Honey nosed round Sam's legs and pushed the door open wider.

"Wow, she got up the stairs fast," Sam muttered. "She couldn't manage them at all when we first got her. Hey, careful." He caught hold of Honey's collar. "No chewing Isabella's stuff."

Isabella looked round her room. Honey didn't come upstairs very often and she hadn't puppy-proofed it.

There *were* quite a lot of things on the floor…

"Can I sit down?" Sam asked and Isabella nodded. She was still confused by this suddenly friendly Sam. She eyed him cautiously as he sat on the floor and pulled Honey into his lap.

"Does she want this?" Isabella asked shyly, holding out a scrunched-up ball of paper.

"Oh, yeah, excellent." Sam reached for it and offered it to Honey, who started to worry at the paper with tiny growls. "It's going to end up shredded all over your floor, though."

"That's OK."

They sat in embarrassed silence for a moment, while Honey growled and scrabbled at the paper ball. Then Sam sighed. "So, I talked to my dad. He noticed that I was upset yesterday. I shouldn't have said those things."

Isabella opened and shut her mouth, and eventually just shrugged. She didn't know what to say.

"I know you weren't really trying to take Honey off me. I was kind of worried about something else...

Did you know I'm going to stay with my mum when the summer holidays start?"

Isabella looked thoughtful. "I think my mum said something about it."

"Yeah, for a fortnight. Which is a long time. I mean, I want to see her but the thing is, I can't take Honey." Sam ducked his head to rub his cheek against the puppy's ears.

"Oh, that is a long time. Um… Why can't you take her?"

"Because my mum's flat is tiny and there's no garden. It's right in the middle of the town too. It's so busy round there. And my dad's taking me on the train, Honey wouldn't like that either." He sighed and hugged Honey tighter. "Anyway … I'm going to have to leave Honey here. So … you can see why I was upset? But actually –" Sam took a deep breath – "actually it's a good thing Honey likes you because it means you can help Dad look after her. He's promised to make a big fuss over her so she doesn't feel like she's been abandoned but he's always so busy with work."

"I'll help," Isabella said eagerly. She

got up and came to sit next to him, leaning against her bed. "I'd love to. And I can see why you said that stuff. I do know Honey's your dog … I'd never try to make her mine. I can show her photos of you, or something…"

Sam snorted. "She'd probably just eat them!" But he sounded a bit happier, Isabella thought, and Honey seemed to think so too — she was looking lovingly up at Sam and beating her tail against his leg.

Chapter Four

Honey stuck her nose curiously
into the bag and sniffed around. It
smelled of Sam. She wondered what
he was doing, squashing all his things
inside – a couple of pairs of shoes, a
tattered book. She could smell food
too – a packet of something sweet and
delicious. She put her paws up on the
side of the bag so she could get further

in and sniff everything properly.

Then she squeaked in surprise as
something soft landed on top of her
and everything went dark. Crossly,
she wriggled out from underneath it,
shaking her ears and looking around to
see what had happened.

"Oops, sorry, Honey." Sam picked up
the hoodie he'd thrown on top of the
bag, looking guilty. "I didn't see you.
Are you OK?" He crouched down and
rubbed the puppy's head. "You can't
get in there. I wish you could come
with me, but you wouldn't like it." He
sighed.

Honey wasn't sure what was going
on but Sam's voice sounded worried
and sad. She edged round the bag
and tried to climb into his lap to

snuggle up with him.

"Are you trying to cheer me up?" Sam sniffed, and then laughed as Honey shoved her nose in his ear. "It's all right, Honey. I'm looking forward to seeing Mum. And Dad and Isabella have promised to look after you."

Honey looked round as Mike shouted from downstairs. "Sam! Are you nearly ready? Come on, we have to head for the station soon."

Sam gave her a hug. "Bye, Honey. See you soon."

Honey followed Sam to the door, getting under his feet as he struggled with the big bag. She went cautiously down the stairs after him, hopping from step to step. She was better at getting up the stairs but somehow they seemed loads steeper on the way down. When she arrived at the bottom, everyone in the house was there. Isabella and her mum were hugging Sam, and Mike was taking out Sam's bag to the car. Honey stood watching them, her ears twitching worriedly. Sam was going somewhere… She stumbled down the last step, ready to dart after him.

"Hey, Honey, you stay here," Isabella said, coming to sit next to her. "No dashing out of the front door."

Honey gave Isabella's hand a quick lick but she was still watching Sam. There was something wrong, she could feel it. Sam left the house all the time but this seemed different. She didn't trust that big bag, and she whined anxiously as Sam went to the door. He looked round at her and waved, then he shut the door behind him.

What was happening? Honey howled – a long, miserable, frightened wail.

Isabella been looking forward to fussing over Honey and giving her loads of love and attention while Sam was away. She'd been confident she could stop the little dog missing Sam but it turned out to be much harder than she'd thought. Every so often, Honey would stop and look around for him, as though she thought he was only in the next room. If anyone mentioned his name, she'd get really excited and run to the door. Isabella got very good at making up silly chase games with Honey's toys, to distract her.

During the week she and Mike went on long walks with Honey, early in the morning before it got too hot. Mum came too, when she wasn't at work. They usually went to the park but they did go back to Sam's favourite woods once, to splash in the stream.

Mike showed Isabella how to make
a dam out of sticks and mud, so that
the tiny stream built up
into a pool. They had
to take it apart
before they
went home
again but
Honey loved
having her
own little
paddling
pool. She kept
putting her nose under the water and
then she would pop up with a confused
look and make huge snorting noises.
Then she shook herself dry all over
Isabella and Mike.

The first weekend Sam was away,

Mum and Mike took Isabella and Beatrice to a country show that was being held in a big field just outside the town. The girls had been looking forward to it for ages, especially as dogs were allowed so Honey could come too. There were farm animals to look at, as well as lots of stalls and displays and a competition tent with cakes and jams and things people had made. Isabella had entered Best Potato Person, with a fluffy-eared potato dog that looked like Honey. When they walked round the tent to look at everything, she found a rosette on it saying second prize.

"You should have won first!" Beatrice said, eyeing the potato fairy that had come first. "Yours is much better."

"Can you pose next to it with Honey, Isabella?" Mike suggested, taking out his phone. "We can send the photo to Sam."

Isabella nodded happily but then she saw that Honey's head was up. The puppy was looking around eagerly, her tail wagging and her eyes bright. She'd heard Mike say Sam's name and she thought he was coming. It was hard to smile for the photo when Honey looked so lost.

"Not much longer," she whispered to Honey as they wandered through the fair. "One more week and he'll be home."

"Oh, there's a dog show!" Beatrice pointed at a signboard by the big show-ring. "You could enter Honey! I bet she'd win waggiest tail!"

Isabella looked down at the puppy, frowning. "I don't think she would at the moment…" Honey wasn't wagging her tail at all. Her head was drooping and Isabella had never seen her look so sad.

Beatrice crouched on the grass next to the puppy. "Poor Honey… Do you think all the people are scaring her?"

Isabella ran her hand gently along Honey's back. "No. I think she's missing –" She turned her head away from the puppy and dropped her voice to a whisper – "Sam. She heard Mike say his name."

"Oh, Honey…" Beatrice said quietly. "Isn't there any way we can cheer her up?"

"I can't think of anything," Isabella said gloomily. "I'd buy her a hot dog with my pocket money if that would make her feel better but she just walked past a whole load of chips someone dropped without even looking. Usually she'd be trying to gobble them all up." She made a face at Beatrice. "It's another whole week till he's back. That's a long time for a puppy to be miserable."

"Maybe he could talk to her on the phone?" Beatrice suggested.

Isabella looked thoughtful. "Yes, I bet she'd recognize his voice. Oh! Even better! He could video call her! Then she'd be able to see him as well. You'd love that, Honey, wouldn't you?" Isabella crouched down to give the mournful puppy a hug.

Honey lifted her paw and scratched at Sam's bedroom door again. She had tried looking for him in his room before and he hadn't been there, but he had to be *somewhere*. Mike had been talking about him when they'd been out – she'd heard him say Sam's name. That must mean Sam was close by?

"He's not there, Honey. But we're going to make sure you can see him soon."

Isabella had followed her upstairs. Honey glanced at her and then back at the door. Her tail drooped. She couldn't hear anyone in the room. It was quiet. Empty.

"Come on, sweetheart. Come and watch TV with me." Isabella's voice was coaxing and Honey padded towards her, twitching her tail just a little. Isabella was warm, and gentle, and very good at scratching ears, even if it wasn't quite the same as being with Sam.

"Shall I pick you up?" Isabella

suggested, hesitating at the top of the stairs. "You don't like going down, do you?" She scooped Honey into her arms and the puppy nuzzled gratefully under her chin as they headed downstairs to the living room.

"What shall we watch?" Isabella said, curling up at one end of the sofa with Honey in her lap. "A film?"

She turned on the TV and pulled a blanket round them both. Some of the strange unhappiness inside Honey eased as Isabella stroked her, running the fur of Honey's ears between her fingers. The puppy's breathing slowed to a soft wheeze and her eyelids fluttered closed. Her head slumped heavily on Isabella's arm and Honey slept.

Chapter Five

"I've got to get back in a minute," Isabella said. She sat up on the garden bench and peered through Beatrice's kitchen window – she could just see the clock. "Sam's going to video call Mike at twelve, so he can talk to Honey."

"Oh, brilliant!" Beatrice nodded excitedly. "She'll love it. It was so sad seeing how much she missed him the other day."

"I know." Isabella smiled. "I can't wait to see Honey when she realizes it's Sam on the screen! And then it's only a few days till he's back for real." She glanced at the clock again. "Actually, I'd better go now. Sam might call early. Mike said he was really excited about it. He's missed Honey loads too!"

"Yeah, see you! Let me know how it goes."

Isabella opened the garden gate with a wave. "I'll shout for you later," she called back. All the houses along the road were built with a side path that went round to the back garden, so all she had to do was slip out of Beatrice's

gate and through hers. Isabella banged
the gate behind her and hurried into
the house.

"Honey! Hey, Honey, look."

Honey blinked sleepily at Isabella
from her basket, where she'd been
napping.

"It's Sam, Honey. Come and see
him!"

Honey leaped up out of the basket,
looking around eagerly. Sam! Where
was he? Why couldn't she see him?

She plodded back over to her
basket, her head hanging, and curled
up again, with her nose buried in the
cushion. Sam wasn't there and Honey

was starting to wonder if he was ever coming back.

"Aww, she looks so sad. I wasn't sure if she'd actually miss me."

Honey put her head up, puzzled but almost hopeful. That was Sam's voice. It was different – crackly and faraway – but it was definitely him! She stood up in the basket, gazing around cautiously. If Sam was here, why couldn't she see him, or smell him? Why wasn't he down on the floor hugging her? Everyone else was in the kitchen, Mike and Isabella and Isabella's mum, but she still couldn't see Sam.

"I don't think she's worked it out yet," Isabella said, looking at something on the table. "Here, I'll move the laptop so she can see you."

Honey looked on, confused, as Isabella moved something on to the floor in front of her, and then came to sit beside her. "Can you see him, Honey? It's Sam!"

"Honey! Hey!"

It was Sam's voice again but Honey still couldn't find him. There was a strange blurry thing moving on the screen that looked a bit like Sam. She didn't like it. Honey backed away uncertainly. It scared her. The screen smelled sharp and unpleasant and the shape flickered and jerked. She whined, and kept backing up until she bumped into her basket and made herself jump. She let out an unhappy growl and shot across the kitchen to the open back door. She had to get away.

"Oh dear, I don't think Honey understood what was happening," Mike said. "I suppose she's never seen you on a screen. It must have been weird for her. Don't worry, Sam, we'll go and find her and cheer her up. I can throw her ball for her, since she's in the garden."

"I thought she'd like it," Sam said miserably. "I really miss her."

"She misses you too," Isabella said. "If we say your name, she looks for you."

"But Isabella's doing an amazing job looking after her," Mike said. "We've been going on lots of walks."

"And you'll be back in a few days," Isabella's mum put in comfortingly. "She'll see you soon."

"I suppose," Sam said, sighing. "Can you go and find her, Dad? Make sure she's OK. She looked so confused."

"Of course. See you soon, Sam. Get your mum to text me which train you're catching on the way back, all right? Bye!" Mike ended the call and closed the laptop. "Let's go and find Honey. She looked really spooked, poor little thing."

Isabella hurried out into the garden. She was expecting to see Honey flopped underneath the table on the patio – the puppy liked the shade in the hot summer weather – but she wasn't there. Maybe she was hiding under one of the bushes.

"Honey!" Isabella called, looking down the garden.

"You can't see her?" Mike asked, standing in the kitchen doorway. "She's probably gone right to the end." He started to walk down the long strip of grass, shouting for Honey.

He and Isabella both turned hopefully when they heard a scuffling sound. But it was just Beatrice, peering over from next door. There was a bench up against the fence on the other side and Beatrice was standing on it.

"Did Honey like seeing Sam?" she asked.

Isabella shook her head. "She hated it. I wish I'd never suggested it. I don't think she knew what was happening, she looked so confused. And then she ran out into the garden to get away.

So we've come out to play with her and cheer her up. You could come and help, if you like. Mike, can Beatrice come over?"

Mike came walking back up the garden. "Yes, sure. I haven't found Honey yet, though. She must be tucked away somewhere, hiding. I didn't realize the video call would upset her so much."

"I'll just ask my mum," Beatrice called over the fence. "I can come round by the side gate." She disappeared back into her own garden, shouting for her mum.

"I'll make sure it's not locked," Mike said, starting towards the gate, and then he stopped, looking worried. "Hang on, it's open!"

"What?"
Isabella
rushed along
the patio to
look. Mike
was right –
the gate was
standing open
and she could
see all the way
up the path
to the front of
the house. "But
Honey…"

"Don't panic," Mike said, but
Isabella thought he sounded as if he
was panicking a bit. "It doesn't mean
she's gone out there. She could still be
hiding somewhere in the garden."

"But she isn't," Isabella said. "You looked everywhere. We called. She comes when we call. She isn't there."

Beatrice appeared in the gateway, beaming at them, but then her smile faded. "What's the matter?"

"The gate… The gate was open!" Isabella cried, darting past her friend and up the path to the front of the house. Her heart was thumping and she felt cold all over. What if Honey had run out on to the road? There was no fence along the front of the house, there was just a gravel driveway. That was why everyone was so careful about not letting Honey dash out of the front door. "Honey!" she called. "Honey, where are you?"

"Honey!" Mike and Beatrice had

come up the path behind her, and Mike was kneeling down to check if the puppy was hiding under the car. "Not there." He hurried out to the pavement and looked up and down the road. "I can't see any sign of her. Maybe I'll go and check the back garden again. We'd feel silly if we went searching for her and she was lurking behind the shed the whole time."

Isabella looked at Mike, her eyes wide with horror. "I think I let her out. I ran round the side of the house from Beatrice's, because I wanted to be back when Sam called. I must not have shut the gate properly. I didn't stop to check that the latch clicked. You said always make sure it clicks!"

"It's OK, Isabella, don't worry." Mike

chewed his bottom lip. "It was an accident. Just one of those things. The gate didn't catch. It doesn't sometimes. Hey, don't cry! No one's cross with you. It's all right."

"It's not all right," Isabella gulped. "Sam wanted me to look after Honey, and now she's run away and it's all because of me!"

Chapter Six

Honey pressed herself against a garden wall as a car rushed past. She wasn't scared of cars when she was out with Sam or Isabella or Mike but everything felt so different now she was all on her own.

She looked back up the road. She could just see the house and for a moment she wondered about going home. Then she shivered. She knew she couldn't bear to see that strange trembling picture again. *That* wasn't Sam.

Where was he, though? She had definitely heard him. He'd said her name! She knew he wasn't in the house but she was sure he must be somewhere close by.

Honey put her nose down and sniffed, looking for any traces. The fences and walls and lamp posts she'd passed were covered in layers of smells, and Honey loved to investigate them whenever they went out. She could pick out her own scent from all their walks, as well as other dogs and Isabella – and, yes, there was Sam's scent too but it was old and stale.

What should she do? Hearing Sam's voice had made her miss him more than ever. She wanted him to be sitting on the living-room floor so she could flop over his legs while he played video games. She loved to snooze like that, just opening one eye when he shouted at the screen. Honey whined, remembering. She wanted to be with Sam so much.

She sniffed again and caught a faint

scent of leaves and damp earth. Her tail twitched into a wag.

The woods!

"Any luck?" Isabella's mum asked anxiously as Isabella and Beatrice ran along the road towards her.

"No." Isabella's voice shook as she answered. She still couldn't believe she'd left the gate open. How could she have been so careless?

Mike came hurrying up. He'd been checking down the other end of the road, towards the park, while the girls knocked on the neighbours' doors and Mum checked the street. "Did you go all the way to the corner?"

Mum nodded. "I kept on calling for her. I suppose she could have gone further," she said doubtfully. "It hasn't been all that long, though, she can't have been gone more than, what, half an hour?"

Mike ran a hand through his hair and sighed. "I just don't know where to look. There are so many places she could be hiding. I keep checking my phone, hoping someone's found her and they'll ring the number on her collar."

"We'd better get you back home, Beatrice," Mum said, looking at her watch. "It'll be your lunchtime."

"It's all right. Mum won't mind," Beatrice started to say, but then she spotted her mum standing on her front door step, waving to them.

"Did you go for a walk?" she called, looking puzzled.

"It's Honey," Mike explained. "We were out looking for her. She slipped out of the garden, you see."

Isabella stood half behind her mum. She couldn't bear to explain to anyone else that she had been the one who'd left the gate open.

"Oh no… Why don't you put a message on the neighbourhood WhatsApp group?" Beatrice's mum suggested. "Someone down the road did that when their cat disappeared a couple of weeks ago, do you remember? It turned out he was shut up in a garage."

"Good idea. I'll do that now," Mike said, reaching for his phone. He smiled at Isabella and Mum. "Why don't you grab some lunch? I'm going to keep looking for a bit."

"I'll come back and carry on looking after lunch. I can, can't I, Mum?" Beatrice asked.

Her mum nodded. "Of course. Don't look so worried, Isabella. I'm sure you'll find Honey soon."

But even though they kept on
searching all afternoon, there was
no sign of the puppy. None of the
neighbours had seen her either –
she seemed to have disappeared
completely. Mum had to go to work
after a while and Beatrice could only
help for an hour after lunch, then she
had to go and see her grandma, but
Mike and Isabella walked for hours.
They went all round the streets,
peering under cars and into front
gardens, calling Honey's name over
and over again.

They were heading back along their
own road when Mike's phone beeped
and Isabella looked up hopefully.

Mike shook his head. "Just someone promising to let us know if they see her." He sighed. "Come on. Let's go and have some dinner, shall we? I know you probably don't feel like it but I bet you didn't eat much lunch."

"Neither did you. Mum made you a sandwich and you didn't even stop to eat it." Isabella sniffed. "What are we going to tell Sam?" She'd been thinking about that all afternoon, in between worrying about Honey.

Mike put his arm round her. "Hopefully we're not going to have to tell him anything. She's not been missing that long, Isabella. Although if we don't find her by tomorrow, then yes, I'll have to call him." He crouched down to look her in the eye. "Honestly, Isabella love, it's not your fault. I should have put a new latch on the gate. You mustn't be upset about it."

"I don't want to stop looking," Isabella whispered.

"I know but we've been walking for hours, Isabella. You look shattered, you're practically falling over your feet. We can heat up some of that lasagne I made yesterday."

"I could make some posters while you're doing that?" Isabella suggested. "Mum lets me use her laptop."

"Good idea! We can put them up in the morning, if we still haven't found her."

Back at the house, Isabella found Mum's laptop in the living room and opened it up. Mum had a file of photos and there were some good pictures of Honey. Isabella chose one where she was looking particularly fluffy and cute. People would make more effort to look out for Honey if they could see how little and sweet she was, wouldn't they? She typed LOST across the top of the page and swallowed hard. How could she have been so careless?

Isabella added a description of Honey, and then Mike's phone number and Mum's too. Then she wrote *Please help us find her!* She printed ten copies, just to start with, and went back into the kitchen to show them to Mike.

"Let's see." Mike sighed as he admired the photo of Honey. "Sorry, Isabella. It's great … for a moment I'd just forgotten how little she is."

"I know," Isabella said, her voice very small.

Mike smiled at her. "Come on. Let's have some food."

Isabella was tired – almost too tired to eat. She kept stabbing her fork into the lasagne and pushing bits around. Then she looked at the food going cold on her plate and thought sadly that Honey would probably love it. The puppy wouldn't have had anything to eat since the morning. She must be so hungry. Eventually Isabella managed to swallow a few mouthfuls and then she looked up at Mike.

"Yeah, I'm not feeling hungry either. Ready to go back out? I thought we could try the park again. There's always lots of dogs being walked about this time of the evening. Maybe she wanted to find some friends."

Isabella nodded but she could tell that Mike was forcing himself to sound cheerful. They didn't really have any idea where Honey might have gone.

"Do you think she could find her way home?" she asked as they headed down the road towards the park. "Dogs are supposed to be good at that."

"I don't know. I hope so but she's only a puppy…"

They were both silent after that, walking and watching, and every so often calling for Honey. That afternoon, they'd been shouting her name eagerly every few seconds, as if they expected her to leap out and come dashing over to them. Now when they called neither of them sounded very hopeful.

At last Mike said, "I think we need

to head back, Isabella. I know it's not dark yet but it's nearly eight."

"But Honey…" Isabella protested. How could they leave her out all night?

"I know." Mike sighed. "I just don't think we're doing any good. We'd be better off getting some sleep and having more energy to look for her in the morning. Maybe you and Beatrice can put those posters up."

The posters that he'd been hoping they wouldn't have to use, Isabella thought miserably. She trailed after Mike back to the house. She hated how quiet it was when they opened the front door. No Honey rushing to greet them, squeaking and snuffling and trying to lick them all over. The house seemed so empty without her.

Chapter Seven

Honey was tracking along a narrow pathway – one that she thought she remembered from walks with Sam. It had a high, earthy bank all along one side, riddled with interesting little holes. If she hadn't been so desperate to find Sam, she would have stopped and tried to dig... But she had more important things to think of. She had been out here a long time now. Sam would be wondering where she was and so would Isabella. She'd seen a few people – several of them had stopped to make a fuss of her. One man had tried to catch her collar but she'd darted away into the trees and he'd sighed and continued with his walk.

She shook her ears briskly and trotted on, snuffling every so often at piles of leaves or fallen branches for Sam's scent. She was so busy sniffing at a tall clump of grass by the side of the path that she didn't spot a plump grey squirrel dashing down a tree trunk. The squirrel raced across the path in front of her and then pulled up short, staring at her in horror.

Honey froze, unsure what she was supposed to do. She'd never seen a squirrel so close up – she could see it breathing, its tiny chest heaving in and out. The squirrel seemed as shocked as she was. It chittered furiously at her for a moment and then shot away up a tree on the other side of the path, leaving Honey staring after it.

After the squirrel disappeared,

Honey looked around a little
anxiously. The bright summer light
was fading now and the trees were
full of noises – chirrups and rustling
and the hiss of the wind through
the leaves. She hadn't even noticed
that squirrel. What else was out here,
watching her? Honey shivered, and
the fur around her neck prickled, and
she stood up.

Isabella had been so tired when they got back to the house she'd had to drag herself up the stairs but once she was in bed, she just didn't feel like sleeping. She couldn't seem to find a comfortable way to lie and her bed was too hot. In the end she sat up, leaning against her pillow with her arms wrapped round her knees. She couldn't stop thinking about Honey, out there on her own. She must be so scared. Then there was Sam. He didn't even know that Honey was missing but he was going to get a phone call from his dad in the morning…

And she was supposed to go to sleep!

Isabella got out of bed and pulled

on the clothes she'd been wearing earlier and a hoodie, because it was cooler now. It was still quite light outside. Mike would be downstairs, waiting for Mum to get home from work. They could go up and down their road one last time. Mike had only stopped them searching because he thought she was tired. What if Honey had been scared and hiding somewhere? Now that most people had gone home and it was quieter, she might decide to come back out. They mustn't miss her!

Isabella hurried downstairs to talk to Mike but when she went into the living room, she saw that he was fast asleep on the sofa, snoring faintly. She stood in the doorway, wondering what to do. She started forwards, meaning to wake him, but then she couldn't bring herself to do it.

It was my fault, so I should sort it out, she thought. *I could go and put those posters up at the same time ... Mum wouldn't mind that. I'm only going down the road.*

Actually, Isabella was pretty sure Mum *would* mind but she was too worried about Honey to think about that. She slipped out of the house through the back door. That meant going through the side gate, which made her eyes fill with tears. Isabella stopped for a moment, blinking hard and looking at Beatrice's gate. Maybe Beatrice could come with her to put up the posters? No. She shook her head – it was too late. Beatrice's mum wouldn't let her go out now.

Just like mine wouldn't... Isabella hurried guiltily up the side path and flitted along the street, taping the posters on to lamp posts. She'd stuck up almost all of them when she came to the little alley that led through to the woods. She stopped dead.

The woods! They hadn't searched there!

Mike almost always walked Honey in the park, Isabella realized. Obviously he hadn't thought of the little path through to Bell's Copse when they'd been searching and she hadn't either. She tucked the sticky tape and the leftover posters into her hoodie pockets and started down the alley.

It wasn't yet dark but the high fences shut out some of the light and Isabella found herself half running towards the woods, although she knew it would be darker in among the trees.

I don't care, she told herself firmly. *I bet Honey's scared on her own in the dark too. I'm going to find her.* She felt almost certain now. How could they have forgotten to search the woods? Honey loved them and so did Sam. Of course she would run to the woods if she was upset or frightened. If she was looking for Sam.

The tall grass in the clearing was looking dry and limp as Isabella crossed it but the woods still had that cool smell of damp new growth. Isabella pulled her hoodie round her more tightly and plunged into the dimness under the trees.

It was getting darker, and there was still no sign of Sam. Honey thought that she must be getting close to the stream, but it was hard to remember all the twisting paths. Should she carry on and look for him down there by the water? She padded on, sniffing for the fresh smell of the stream, but she couldn't catch it on the air. Perhaps it wasn't this way after all… She whined uncertainly. The woods felt bigger without Sam or Isabella, and darker.

A loud growling some way behind her on the path sent Honey into a sudden frightened crouch, huddling against the earthy bank. Was it another dog? Why did it sound so angry?

There was an answering shout – "No, Bertie. No! Leave the squirrel alone!" – followed by more growling, and a fierce scrabbling and scuffling of paws.

Honey looked frantically back and forth, wondering what to do. She didn't want to be anywhere near that dog, or the woman shouting. She scurried along the path but she could still hear the woman talking crossly to the dog. "What have you found now? No more chasing squirrels, Bertie."

Honey felt the wood grow quiet. She could *hear* the other dog listening. She felt the curious silence, and then suddenly there were heavy paws thumping along the path and deep eager breathing.

The other dog was following her.

Honey sped up and then she spotted a dark hollow in the bank, where the roots of a great tree had come creeping down. The earth had been washed

away by years of
rain, leaving a
hole just big
enough for a
frightened
little dog.
Honey
tucked
herself inside,
trying not to sneeze
as loose earth rained down
around her ears.

Where was Sam? Where was
Isabella? Honey watched, mouse-quiet,
as the dog came stomping closer.

Chapter Eight

Isabella hadn't thought about other people being in the woods but she supposed it was a popular place for an evening walk, especially after such a hot a day. She nearly asked a woman pulling a huge dog if she'd seen Honey but then she thought that she'd better not. For a start, the woman and the dog both looked grumpy, and Mum wouldn't want her talking to strangers anyway. The woman with the dog would probably be shocked that Isabella was out alone this late too. She might think Isabella was lost and she ought to take her home. Isabella slipped off the path and ducked behind a huge straggly holly bush, waiting for them to walk past.

"No more chasing things, Bertie! I think that was a rabbit, poor little thing. You're a great big monster. Come on, home!"

Isabella watched them stomp by. She shivered as the silence settled over the woods again. She wasn't lost, not exactly, but it was weird how different the paths looked in the dim evening light. When the woman with the dog had gone, Isabella came back out on to the path and looked around uncertainly. It was getting colder. And the shadows were deeper. She found that she was clutching tightly at her arms and gave herself a shake.

"Stop it," she muttered out loud. "You're supposed to be looking for Honey." She marched along the path. She couldn't get lost if she stuck to this same one, could she? "Honey!" she called, trying hard to keep her voice from wobbling. "Here, girl! Honey!" But however loud she tried to shout, her voice sounded thin and faint in the old woods. The trees seemed to be pressing closer in on the path, growing taller and darker, and Isabella's voice shivered away.

Something chattered sharply in the trees above her and Isabella whirled round, squeaking with fright. What was it? There was a scurrying, like little claws, and she saw a squirrel race along a branch.

Just a squirrel! It was silly to be scared of such a tiny creature but she couldn't help it. Her heart felt as if it was swinging about inside her and she was cold all over.

Another scuffling noise further up the path – something down on the ground this time – made her press her hands against her mouth. She imagined a fox, or maybe a huge fierce dog, or even a wolf – although she knew that was stupid. Isabella almost shut her eyes, so she didn't have to see what it was but what good would that do? Whatever it was would just be able to eat her more easily… She clenched her fingernails tightly into her palms and forced herself to look.

Wriggling out from under a knot of tree roots at the foot of the bank was a dusty, scruffy, golden dog.

"Honey!" Isabella yelped, crouching down and opening her arms – and Honey shot into them, trembling and whining.

Honey nestled against Isabella's shoulder, pressing her nose into the place between Isabella's chin and her neck. She could smell that Isabella had

been scared too,
but it was all right
now they were
together.

Isabella might
not be Sam, but
she was kind and
she scratched ears
well, and she
smelled of home.

"We've been looking for you
all day," Isabella was murmuring, as she
stumbled back up the path with Honey
in her arms. "Have you been out here
in the woods all this time? We should
have looked here earlier."

Honey felt Isabella's heart thump
a little harder as they came into the
narrow alleyway that led back to the

road and she nuzzled close, swiping Isabella's chin with her tongue and making her giggle.

"It's OK," Isabella said. "The alley isn't very long. It just feels a bit spooky. There!" She sighed. "Back on our road now." She was silent for a moment as they hurried along and then she added, "I wonder if Mike woke up... I suppose even if he did, he wouldn't know I went out. Maybe we can tell him and Mum tomorrow. I don't know."

Honey snuffled in Isabella's ear. She didn't understand what Isabella was saying but Isabella sounded anxious.

"No, we can't do that," Isabella murmured. "It would be mean. I don't want Mike going to bed thinking you're still lost. Or Mum. I bet she's been worrying about you all the way through her shift. We can't not tell them, that's silly."

As they reached the house, Honey tensed and then struggled in Isabella's arms, remembering the strange version of Sam she'd seen earlier on.

"Hey, careful!" Isabella stopped, looking down at Honey worriedly. "What is it? Oh… I bet you're still upset about that video call." She swallowed. "He's not here, Honey. But he's coming home in a few days, I promise. Not long to wait." She crouched down and put Honey on the gravel, keeping hold of her collar, and Honey eyed the house doubtfully.

"I don't want to take you inside, not

if you're scared," Isabella whispered. "What shall we do, Honey?"

Honey tugged uncertainly at Isabella holding her collar. She didn't quite know what she wanted. Not to go back to the woods, she was sure of that. She had spent a long time huddling under those roots until the other dog had gone, frightened by every noise and breath of wind. When she'd seen Isabella on the path she'd been so grateful, so relieved.

Isabella wasn't going to let anything hurt her, Honey decided. She tugged again, pulling Isabella towards the house, and saw her smile.

"Let's go round the side and in the back door. I don't want to wake up Mike by ringing the bell…"

When they got there, Isabella pushed the door open and they both peered into the kitchen cautiously. As soon as Honey saw her food bowl she remembered how hungry she was. She pulled herself out of Isabella's grip and dashed to stand by it, looking up at Isabella hopefully.

"I forgot you must be starving! Here."

Honey watched, tail wagging, as Isabella pulled out the food bag from the cupboard and filled her bowl, then rinsed out and refilled her water bowl too. Honey ate greedily, gulping down her food to ease the aching hunger inside her.

"Good girl," Isabella murmured. "Oh, I've just had an idea. Stay there a minute."

Honey didn't even notice her darting out of the kitchen. She gobbled up every scrap of her late dinner and slumped wearily on to the floor by her bowl. Then she glanced round at last, surprised to see that Isabella had gone. She stood up again uncertainly, all the strangeness rushing back.

"It's OK! It's OK, Honey, look."
Isabella hurried back in. "Were you
scared? Look, I brought you this." She
crouched down by Honey's basket,
laying something inside.

Honey padded over cautiously to see
what it was. She sniffed at the faded
old sweatshirt and then sniffed again
in delight when she recognized the
smell.

"It's the one Sam wears as a pyjama
top sometimes," Isabella explained,
arranging it in a ball at the side of
Honey's basket. "I reckon it has to
smell like him. Is that nice? I went
upstairs to get it and I wanted to see
where Mike was. He's still asleep on
the sofa, Honey! So I left a note on

the coffee table. Mum's going to be so upset with me in the morning but I got you back, so maybe she'll let me off. Night night, Honey."

Isabella ran one hand gently down the puppy's back and Honey shivered with pleasure. She was home and full and sleepy, and she had Sam's sweater. She watched, her nose resting on the edge of the basket as Isabella tiptoed out of the kitchen. She could hear her going quietly up the stairs. If she listened carefully enough, she could hear Mike faintly snoring in the living room.

Honey shook herself and stood up. She didn't want to be on her own. She stumbled out of her basket, dragging the sweater with her, and set off through the kitchen and up the stairs. At last she clambered exhaustedly on to the landing and padded into Isabella's room.

"Hey! What is it?" Isabella whispered as Honey scrambled up on to the bed. "Did you come to find me?" She giggled. "And you brought Sam's jumper."

The puppy stretched out next to Isabella, the sweater huddled up between her paws. She was home and safe…

"So what did Dad say the next morning?" Sam asked as they headed along the path through the woods for their first walk since he got back home. He was smirking and Isabella shrugged.

"Nothing. I think he was a bit embarrassed that he slept through me sneaking out *and* back in again." She sighed. "My mum had a lot to say, though. She made me swear I'd never, ever go out on my own ever, ever, ever again. And she wouldn't let me go over to Beatrice's. I'm surprised she's letting me go out with you. Look, that's where Honey was, tucked under those roots."

"Wow…" Sam crouched down to

look and watched Honey sniffing at the hole cautiously. "She remembers, I reckon. Look at her. It's OK, Honey. I'm not going away again for ages, I promise." He smiled at Isabella. "Thanks for looking after her."

"I let her get out!" Isabella stared at him. "And it was my fault she was so upset in the first place. I looked it up on Mum's laptop – some dogs really don't like seeing people they know on screens because they don't see the same way we do. You must have looked really strange to her."

"Yeah, maybe. But you were trying to cheer her up. And when she ran away, you got her back again. You didn't give up."

"I suppose…" Isabella leaned down

to stroke Honey, and the little dog stopped investigating the hole under the roots and put her front paws up on Isabella's knees, panting happily. "I was so scared. It made it even worse that she's your puppy and I'd lost her. I had to find you, didn't I?" She rubbed Honey's ears and laughed as the puppy licked her nose.

"She's your puppy too," Sam said, and Isabella smiled at him.

There in the dappled sun under the trees, with Honey scrabbling lovingly at her shorts, Isabella thought that maybe he was right.

HOLLY WEBB

Holly Webb started out as a children's book editor and wrote her first series for the publisher she worked for. She has been writing ever since, with over one hundred books to her name. Holly lives in Berkshire, with her husband and three children. Holly's pet cats are always nosying around when she is trying to type on her laptop.

For more information about Holly Webb visit:

www.holly-webb.com